South Porcupine

Jem's Island

Jem's Island

story by **Kathryn Lasky**

pictures by **Ronald Himler**

SCHOLASTIC INC.
New York Toronto London Auckland Sydney

Text copyright © 1982 by Kathryn Lasky.
Illustrations copyright © 1982 by Ronald Himler.
All rights reserved. Published by Scholastic Inc., 730 Broadway, New York, NY 10003, by arrangement with Charles Scribner's Sons, an imprint of Macmillan Publishing Company.
Printed in the U.S.A.
ISBN 0-590-46422-1

2 3 4 5 6 7 8 9 10   23   99 98 97 96 95 94 93

For Chris
Paddler of a thousand miles
K.L.

1

It came back to him in the winter night—that rhythm. Lying on the top bunk, Jem raised his arms toward the ceiling and gripped the imaginary double-blade paddle. Dropping his left wrist, he rotated it one quarter turn in the other hand, feathered, and dipped silently into the water. The room was thick with sleep and the soft snores of his younger brother in the lower bunk. But Jem was awake and paddling in the top bunk. Through a winter night the summer rhythms came back, the strokes that his father had taught him, the strokes that drew the kayak through the water. Slender and like a polished mahogany needle, the boat they called *Wasso* slipped through that water. He did not hear his brother in the lower bunk. The framework of the double-decker beds melted into darkness, and Jem saw instead wings of spray flying in silver symmetry off the bow as *Wasso* sliced through the chop of the bay.

That's the way it would be next summer, when he and his dad took their camping trip. If he could only wait! But summer was five months away. Deer Isle and Penobscot Bay seemed a million miles from Cleveland. Why, Jem muttered, did I have to be born in Cleveland?

If he had to wait five months for his first overnight kayak trip to an island, he could at least read about his dad's trip of twenty years ago—the big trip, the voyage. Voyage? Trip? *Wasso* would take Jem and his father no more than twenty-five miles to and from an island, round trip. But the same kayak had carried his dad and his uncle Peter a thousand miles from Skagway, Alaska, to Seattle, Washington. A thousand miles is a voyage. Twenty-five miles is a trip, Jem guessed. But still, he could hardly wait. And it would be just he and his dad. Not Michael, not Jessica, not his mom. Just he and his dad. He turned on the lamp and opened the faded loose-leaf notebook. First there was the picture, the wobbly diagram of the kayak, an aerial view of the boat without its deck, showing stowage

space. The drawing was captioned "The World's Largest Three-Dimensional Jigsaw Puzzle." It was like assembling a jigsaw puzzle to fit in all the gear that the two brothers needed for sixty days in the wilderness. Cooking utensils, sleeping bags, food, books, charts, tools, cameras, spare parts. Two hundred pounds of gear in all had to fit into the twenty-foot kayak. Jem and his father would need only a fraction of this gear. Fitting it in would be no problem, but still Jem loved studying this diagram because if you had a plan, even things that seemed impossible could become adventures. Real adventures, he had decided, had plans.

Everyone had said twenty years ago that Ben Gray and his brother Peter couldn't do it, would never survive the thousand-mile journey along the rugged and desolate coast with its treacherous tides that could suck them straight out to sea. But the southeast coast of Alaska was the ultimate challenge for expert kayakists like the two brothers. And twenty years ago Ben and Peter Gray were the first to attempt it, at least in recorded history.

Jem opened the journal and began to read. The journal was full of wonderful, true stories, like the one about the killer whales that trailed the kayak for ten minutes. And it was full of great places with names like Tracy Arm, Meyer's Chuck, and Taku Harbor. And there were people in the journal, too, whose names were stories in themselves: Lonesome Pete and Halibut Pete and Tiger Olsen. There were true tales of a coastline where hundreds of eagles still flew, of fantastically shaped icebergs, of ghost towns and gold panners.

Jem's trip this summer would be no voyage; he didn't kid himself about that. There were no killer whales in Penobscot Bay. But there were dolphins, and it was beautiful. Hurry up and wait!

Jem shut the book and turned off the light.

2

Jem pored over chart number 309 of East Penobscot Bay on the porch of their cabin that foggy summer morning. Stinson's Neck on the chart looked more like a witch riding a broomstick than an island. And Pickering Island looked like a seagull plunging out of the sky for a fish. Some of the islands, like Saddleback and Great Spoon, looked like what they were called. But Jem wondered about other islands that had been named for reasons apart from their shapes. These were the "Once-upon-a-time" islands. That's what his mom had said. They had real stories and almost real stories connected with them, and that is how they came by their names.

Deer Isle, where Jem and his family spent the summer, was a once-upon-a-time island, for once there had been more deer than people on the island. But the high ledge on which the Gray family cabin perched had been named the Giant's Chair. The cabin was on the top of the chair back. Thirty feet below, a slab of pink rock formed the seat which slid into the sea. Hog Island, to the east of Deer Isle, certainly didn't look like a hog. There must be a story there, Jem thought. But the south part of the island was called Devil's Head, and if you looked at it a certain way—Jem cocked his head so that his eyes read it northeast to southwest—it did look a little like a devil's head.

"Do you think that looks like a devil's head, Michael?"

"No. I think it looks like an atomic starblaster."

"Is that all you ever think about—galactic warfare?"

"Well, all you think about is kayak trips to islands!"

The screen door opened. "Fog bored or fog bound?"

"I'm not bored, Mom. I find Michael boring!"

"And I find you boring, with all your plans for your big trip. You'd think you were going to Alaska or something. Well, you're not!"

Liza Gray saw the hurt in Jem's eyes. "Come on, Michael. Come with me. We'll go pick blueberries."

"You can't see them in the fog."

"Come on, Michael." She took his shoulders and steered him firmly inside.

Michael turned as he went through the screen door. "Just remember," he yelled, "you're only going overnight. It's no big-deal trip!"

Jem returned to chart 309. Michael was jealous. He knew that, but he was still mad at his brother. He looked at the chart. He had to figure out where he and his dad would go tomorrow. His father was letting him do most of the planning. He could choose the island. It could be any island as long as they could get there and back within two days. Next year they would take a longer trip, but for this year two days and a night was the limit.

Heart Island was too close. They could come and go in a morning even with the wind against them. It was blowing southeast now. Southeast always brought in the fog. But it would probably turn around to northwest by tomorrow. Northwest was the clearing wind. After eleven summers on Deer Isle, Jem knew something about the ways of the wind on this coast. Northwest would be a following wind, perfect for Isle au Haut or Kimball Island. At twelve miles that was the farthest Jem could imagine going. The kayak's speed was just over three miles an hour. With a following wind it might be closer to four. So they had to plan on four hours to get there. Getting back, if it was still blowing northwest, would take a lot longer, for the wind would be against them, "hard on the nose." A closer choice might be Dagger or Sheep Island, especially if it blew northeast. Jem lined up his hand on the northeast axis of the chart. On the chart these islands didn't appear very interesting. Too round, Jem thought, not enough dents and wiggles in the shoreline. The islands with jagged contours and deep clefts, where the sea furrowed inland, making narrow bays, coves, and miniature fjords, were always the most exciting to explore.

If, however, a northerly wind didn't come, and it blew southwest instead, what then? Maybe Pickering? Too close, Jem thought. Or Hog? Or Chatto? Not Chatto. Chatto was too close to the mainland. He hoped it would blow northwest. Northwest was a good wind. It was crisp and cool, and it cleared.

As Jem was folding up the chart, his little sister Jessica walked out on the porch.

"Are you taking the Pop-Tarts, Jem? Because there's only one left and I want it!"

"No, we're not taking Pop-Tarts."

"Why not? You always eat Pop-Tarts. You've eaten Pop-Tarts for breakfast every morning since you were born."

"Well, I'm not going to eat them on this trip. There's no way to bake them. Besides, they might get soggy. We'll be eating hardtack. That's what sailors eat at sea on long voyages, and Grand Banks fishermen. It doesn't get soggy. Come on, I'll show you."

On the floor of the kitchen under a shelf was a curved-bottom storage case. Jem flipped up the lid. Inside, among other stores, was a box labeled Grimson's Hardtack Bread. Jem opened the box and took out a biscuit. "Here." He handed it to Jessica.

"Ooooh! It's like a little stone muffin. Are you sure you can bite it?"

"Once you crack it open, you can."

"With a hammer?"

"No, a rock will do!" said their father, who had just walked in. "Or you can soak it a bit in salt water."

"I thought you didn't want anything soggy. Why don't you take cereal?"

"We don't want anything that gets soggy before we want it to," Jem said.

"Besides," said Ben, "cereal is for breakfast tables, for everyday. We're going camping."

"Yeah," said Jem, nodding at his plain-speaking dad. He wished his dad had been there when Michael was bugging him.

"What else you got there, Jem?"

"Jam, sugar, coffee for Dad . . ."

"What will *you* drink?"

"Water."

"That's all?"

"Maybe some of that instant grape stuff that you can mix with water, as long as we can get it in a can and not a bag. We got cheese, too."

"That's not cheese," Jessica said.

"It is, too. It's Vermont cheddar."

"Not all cheese is flat and comes in individual cellophane wrappers, Jess," her father said. "Here, try some." Ben un-

wrapped the hunk of cheddar and cut a small piece for Jessica. She took a tiny nibble and crinkled her nose.

"Yuck!"

"It's great! Here, give me some, Dad." Jem ate a wedge of the cheese. "It probably tastes even better with hardtack."

"What will you have for dinner?" Jessica asked.

"Fish or clams—whatever we can catch or dig up or pick. Plenty of berries now, and mackerel are running," Ben said.

"I think you need to take a steak, just in case."

That evening Jem and his father checked over the lists that Jem had printed neatly on two pieces of paper. There were two lists—one for food and one for equipment.

FOOD

hardtack	apples
jam	butter
sugar	coffee
peanut butter	instant grape juice
cheese	chocolate bars
oranges	

It looked pretty short to Jem. He hoped his father was right about the clams, the mackerel, and the berries. The gear list was much longer.

GEAR

fishing tackle	tool kit
clam spade	camera
cooking pot	sleeping bags
skillet	tent
two forks, two spoons	tarp
Swiss army knife	compass
first aid kit	chart
canteens	rain gear
water jugs	books
spare rudder	games?
spare paddle	

"Should we bring cards?" asked Jem.

"Should we?" said his father. "I don't know."

"I guess maybe it's like cereal. We do it all the time here. So maybe I won't take a deck to the island."

"I bought something in town that you might want to take." Jem's dad reached toward the mantle. "Here you go."

He tossed Jem a leather book with a dolphin carved on the front. Inside the book, bound like a notebook with leather thongs instead of rings, were hundreds of blank pages. A book with hundreds of pages is for a voyage, Jem thought, not just a trip. What was his dad thinking?

"Come on. Open it up. Here's a pencil. Time for your first navigation lesson. We need to chart out some possible courses. You say you're thinking about Duck Harbor on Isle au Haut and Kimball Island."

Ben lit another kerosene lamp and spread out chart 322. It looked just like the other chart except there were two compass roses—drawings of the face of a compass—in the parts of the chart that showed open water.

Jem hunched over the chart. His dad moved the lamp closer.

"You see this compass rose, Jem?"

"Um-hmm."

"The outside ring is the ring of true direction, of the geographic location of the North Pole. The inside ring is the magnetic direction. It shows the magnetic North Pole, the one that the compass needle points to. You always plot your course in reference to the inner circle, the magnetic direction. Now take

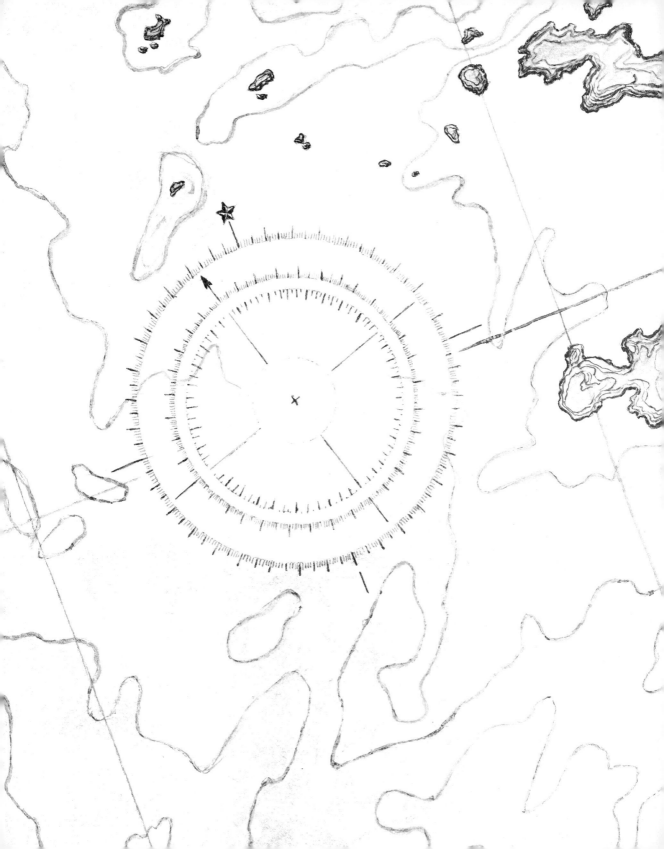

these parallel rules. The first step is to lay them along the straightest sea line between Deer Isle and the island you want to go to. Where's that?"

"Isle au Haut or maybe Kimball's."

"Well, it will be the same line, so you can start."

Jem took the two straightedge transparent rulers. They were numberless and connected in parallel to one another by crosspieces that allowed one to slide in front of the other. He laid them down along the angle of the direction between Deer Isle and Isle au Haut.

"Okay, that's the angle of your course. Now draw a line along your course."

Jem drew a straight line between the two islands.

"Now step the rules toward the compass rose, but keep them at the same angle as your course."

Jem slid the two parallel strips of plastic back and forth, and the rules moved sideways until they were over the compass rose.

"What does it read? Remember, read the inside circle for the magnetic direction. That's the one you want."

"180° south."

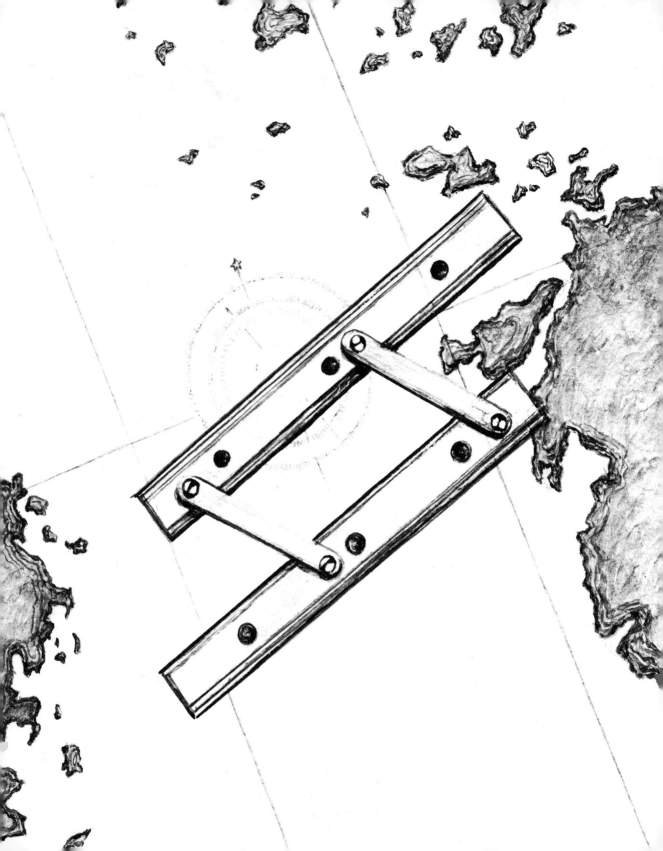

"Okay. Write that down along the line you've drawn, and in your notebook, too. Now you can measure the distance with the dividers."

This Jem knew how to do. He took sharp bronze needles that were joined at the top and opened them up to the three-mile length on the chart's scale. Holding the same width, he measured it off on his course line. "Twelve and a half miles," Jem said.

"Good," his father said. "Add on two miles for rounding Dunham Point. We can follow the coast until then, and then we'll pick up the compass course. To be on the safe side, chart a couple of other courses in case the wind is not northwest and we have to go in another direction."

Jem stayed up another hour charting courses to islands in every direction. He stepped his way with parallel rules across shoals and channels, through the bay to islands called Sparrow and Bear, Scraggy and Bumpkin, Brimstone and Shag, Otter and Colt, Rabbit Ear and Drunkard's Ledge. There was a kind of excitement that Jem felt when he drew these lines and knew that they really meant something, that they could actually guide him to new destinations. The lines turned winter dreams into something real.

3

There was no wind. There was only fog and the sound of lapping water. The summer house slept, but Jem and his father were up carrying gear down to the shore. The kayak rested upside down on the small crescent of beach. It was as beautiful upside down as right side up. The Swedish boat builders who made it loved wood so much that they had seen to it that the grain of the wood was perfectly symmetrical—not just on top where it showed, but on the bottom, too. The boat was strong but light, not much more than fifty pounds unloaded. Jem and his father carried it across the beach and walked barefoot into the bone-aching cold water. Jem slid the curved stowage case into the stern. Its contours were identical to those of the hull. The fit was perfect. This and another stow-

age case like it had been made twenty years earlier by the brothers for their Alaska trip. In between the two seats, under the covered deck, was room for more storage. They packed in their sleeping bags, clothes, and a camera. In the bow, toward the point, the tent had been fitted; behind it, the repair kit and spare parts.

When the last piece of gear was stowed, Jem and his father pulled on their rubber spray skirts. This was the part that makes kayaking different from any other type of boating. This was the part that made it special for Jem. The spray skirts have an elastic hole to fit around the paddler's waist and an elastic outer edge that fits over the rim of the cockpit. It makes a seal between the paddler and the boat so that no water can get in. But the spray covers do more than keep a paddler dry. The spray skirt made Jem a part of the boat and the boat part of him. The outer and inner edges of the spray skirt formed a double ring. Maybe, Jem thought, it was like the double circle of the compass rose with its true direction and magnetic direction.

Jem and his father climbed into their cockpits. There was always that thrilling first motion that Jem felt when he low-

ered himself into the seat and felt the water underneath the keel just inches away. It was in that instant that the boat came alive for Jem, and he felt an extraordinary connection with the most far-off places, for in the water world everything was one and everything seemed possible. In the stern cockpit Jem fitted his spray skirt over the rim, and his father did the same in the bow cockpit. The seal was made, and with one stroke they glided into deeper water. The white fog swallowed them. Only the dip of their paddles could be heard. There were no splashes. A V of ripples streamed back toward Jem as the bow sliced through the still water.

Jem and his dad paddled silently. The fog was so thick that they could not see the coast to follow it to Dunham Point. Instead, they had to use another compass course that Jem had plotted the night before. The compass was mounted on the deck just in front of his father, and Ben Gray steered by pushing with his feet on a bar that was beneath the deck and attached by wires to the rudder in the stern of the boat. Unless the fog lifted, there would be no way of visually knowing when they rounded the point to pick up the new compass course of 180° south. So Jem had worked out the mileage on this coastal course and knew that they had to paddle 250° west-southwest for exactly forty minutes to clear Dunham Point before turning onto their new course for Isle au Haut. It was Jem's job to keep track of the time and call the course change. Somewhere a lobsterman was hauling traps. Jem could tell that the lobsterman was hauling and not traveling by the rhythmic idling of the engine. But the fog blanketed everything, and the engine sounded like the throb of a great muffled heart.

It was an edgeless world they paddled through, without boundaries or perimeters. The water itself seemed almost the same colorless gray of the fog. It could have been either sky or space through which they moved. It was a timeless world, really, except for the forty minutes that Jem had ordered necessary. Now the throb of the engine was swallowed up too by the fog. There was no sound except for the twin dip of their paddles. Jem could listen to his own heart, his own breathing. His arms held strong. They did not tire as they had last summer. He felt he could paddle forever like this, with the paddle striking the rhythm between him and the sea.

Suddenly there was a raw tidal smell. Unmistakably, it

was the strong and slightly sweet odor of wet rocks and sea-weed exposed at low tide. It was the smell that scared the day-lights out of sailors at night or in fog, but in a kayak with its six-inch draft, or depth, there was little need to fear going aground.

"I can smell the point," Ben said.

"Yep. We're right on schedule." Jem looked at his watch. Thirty-eight minutes had passed, and Dunham Point was off their left, or port, side, probably not more than twenty yards. "We paddle straight for two more minutes and then turn on to 180° south."

Exactly two minutes later, when Jem called, "New course," the fog thinned. The rocky point became softly visible, as if it were behind a screen or gauze. On top of one of the point's rocks, like a teacup on a saucer, a seal arched its back, yawked, and slid into the water.

"Seals all around here," Ben said.

As the fog lifted, Jem and his dad became more talkative. The muffled private world of the gray mist evaporated as the sun burned through, and a new world was revealed, with green islands set like small jewels in the sparkling water. Cor-

morants and seagulls cruised effortlessly over *Wasso*. Jem and Ben paddled on, picking up their pace, skimming close to steep-shored islands, under cliffs that cascaded with moss and trees that grew straight out from sheer rock faces, defying gravity. With the shallow depth of the kayak, Jem and his father could glide close enough to touch the rock.

At lunchtime they slid into a slight curve of a beach on South Porcupine Island. Small stones, as smooth and round as coins and polished by a million years of lapping water, covered this beach. Jem and his dad sat down to eat their lunch.

"The hardtack looks just like the stone, Dad."

"Probably as hard, too."

Jem tried to crack a biscuit open. "It is. See? Not a crumb."

"Better find a sharper rock. Try over there." Ben pointed to a place at the edge of the beach.

Jem walked over and began looking. Just as he was picking up a sharp-edged rock from amid the debris of driftwood and seaweed, a wise, calm eye seemed to stare up at him. It was a flat piece of driftwood in the perfect contours of a whale's head, with the likeness of a whale's eye set within. Jem

drew the wood from its rock ledge. A sculptor could not have
carved it better. Gathered in a swirl of wrinkles, the eye was
centered at precisely the right spot in the sea-silvered wood,
which itself was shaped just like a whale from flukes to head.
There were even the fine horizontal lines combing the lower
half of the "body," just like the striations on the underside of a
blue whale.

Jem munched his hardtack and cheese and looked at the
driftwood whale. "For just two people alone on an island," he
said, "this is a pretty noisy lunch. Hardtack has to be one of
the noisiest foods going."

After lunch they dug some clams. It was near low tide then, and by evening it would be high tide, and they wouldn't be able to dig any. They picked a small pail of berries, too, and each ate a handful. Then they climbed back into *Wasso* and slid away, the driftwood whale tucked in under the spray skirt near Jem's leg. Mark, Scraggy, Sparrow, West Halibut slid by. Then came an island between Halibut and Kimball that had no name. Jem had hardly noticed it on the chart. They rounded its stubby headland, and on the underside a cove opened up, surprising Jem and his father. Long and crooked as an old person's finger, the cove appeared to channel far into the island.

"Let's go there," Jem said excitedly.

"Let's do!"

A cormorant seemed to be the only inhabitant of the cove. The following tide gave *Wasso* a slight boost. Jem and his father rested their paddles and coasted quietly up the cove that was full of blind corners and secret turns. It was when they passed the last "knuckle," just before the fingertip, that Jem decided that this was where they should camp. Suddenly Kimball Island and Isle au Haut seemed crowded in comparison to this no-name island with its surprise cove.

"I want to camp here, Dad. Is that okay with you?"

"Fine," Ben said and smiled to himself, remembering from twenty years ago that self-discovered things always seemed better and uncharted places more memorable than charted ones.

ℳ 4 ℳ

They coasted to the tip of the water finger. There was a sand beach. Pink ledges on either side sloped into the water, making shallow, tub-size pools just right for swimming. There was a rock just right for cast fishing and a cliff just right for climbing. It was a place you got to and you knew exactly what you wanted to do. First Jem swam in the pools and then in the larger part of the cove as the sea grass ribboned through his legs. His dad watched from shore.

"How can you stand that cold water, Jem?"

"I just keep my feet on the bottom!" Jem whooped and ducked.

After swimming Jem explored the shoreline. Besides the big rock pools, there were several small tidal pools. Glittering

in the late afternoon sun, they looked like oddly-cut jewels. Each pool was alive with small plants and seaweeds and some with tiny minnows.

Jem and his father climbed the short cliff. On top of the island was a thick grove of spruce. From the water this grove of trees had looked like a crown on the round flat top of the island. Through the trees and out the other side of the grove the land turned brambly with berry bushes. They picked blueberry, raspberry, and blackberry, dropping them into Ben's hat because they had forgotten the pail. Some islands were "picked out" by hikers and boaters, but "No Name," as Jem had begun to call his island, was not lived on or visited or picked from, except by cormorants and seagulls and whatever four-footed animals lived there.

"Lucky we dug those clams on Porcupine," Jem said, as he watched his father pan-fry a ridiculously small mackerel which ordinarily they would have thrown back.

"This is just an hors d'oeuvre. Those clams will be great!" Ben slid the fish onto a tin plate. It looked even smaller. Jessica might have been right—a steak, just in case. "Hand me the rest of the butter. We'll melt it for the clams."

Jem wondered what Jessica, Michael, and his mother were doing now, that very moment. Eating dinner, he guessed. Maybe chowder, maybe hamburgers. He wondered if they wondered what he was doing. They must. Two places were empty at the table. They didn't have a table here. There was a slab of rock that did fine. They had pulled *Wasso* above the high tide line and turned her upside down, and now they sat leaning against her hull. The cove faced west, just like the Giant's Chair. Jem and his dad shared out the mackerel—all four bites of it—and a heap of clams, and watched the sun slide down behind the horizon like a thin gold coin. It was good thinking that he and his dad, and his mom and Jess and Michael were miles apart but watching the same sun slide on down—Jem and Ben from a beach on an island with no name and a rock for a table, the other Grays from a beach on an island called Deer with a pine table.

They had finished their berries. "Tell me a story, Dad. Tell me an Alaska story."

"An Alaska story? I've told you all of them a hundred times."

"I still like to hear them."

"Alaska was one adventure. This is Maine, another adventure. I'll tell you a Maine story."

"Is it true?"

"You bet."

"Good, let's hear it."

"Once upon a time, a long time ago, on Deer Isle . . ."

"Before the bridge to the mainland?"

"Yes, long before the bridge. If there had been a bridge, this story wouldn't have happened. No, it was before I was born and your grandfather was just a few years older than yourself, maybe seventeen or eighteen at the most. The winters were long on an island without a bridge, especially when it was the kind of winter cold enough to ice the channel but not cold enough to make the ice safe for walking across to the mainland. Too thin for feet, too thick for canoes. You think Cleveland is bad. You ought to try an out island in February. Well, March came, and the ice started to break right up, and your grandfather was sure that his charts from the Coast and Geodetic Survey Department had come. He wanted to pick them up."

"The ones for his trip out the St. Lawrence and around the Gaspé Peninsula?"

"That's it, the New England circumnavigation. He'd

45

dreamed of it all winter. He'd ordered the charts just after Christmas, so he was sure they had arrived. That first morning when the ice had just cleared off, no sooner, a herd of low, dark clouds scudded in, and the channel water became choppy as a northeast wind whistled down. My grandfather, your great-grandfather, said 'Looks like a Northeaster, Pete. You going?' And your grandfather, his son, said he thought he could make it across and back before anything got nasty."

"He let him go?"

"Yes."

"Did he warn him or anything?"

"He asked him if he was going."

"So he just let him go like that?"

"Yes."

"What happened?"

"He made it across fine, but on the way back the wind started to build really fast, and by the time he was halfway across, the channel was boiling white—tops of waves blowing right off. My dad was paddling along. If he'd turned around to go back he would have been caught on the side, abeam, and swamped. He would have lived about two minutes in that water. He had no choice but to paddle right into the teeth of this thing. Somehow he made it. When he walked up from the beach to the old farmhouse where our family lived, his dad was standing there on the front porch. He'd watched him come back. His dad's cheeks were all wet, his eyes red. He'd been crying. He never thought his son would make it back."

"Did he kiss him?"

"No. He wasn't the kissy kind. I think Dad told me that he said something like 'Charts still dry, Pete?' "

"Huh." Jem thought a minute. "Do you think he was right to let him go?"

"You have to let go sometime."

"Would you have let me go?"

Ben paused. "I guess if I thought you were a good enough paddler, I really couldn't stop you."

"Did your parents try to stop you when you and Uncle Pete went to Alaska?"

"No, but all their friends in Cleveland thought they should have, thought they were crazy to let us go." Ben laughed softly. "Come on, let's you and me go for a night glide!"

"A 'night glide'? What's a 'night glide'?"

"You can only do it on a night like this. No wind, and the water is as still as a dark mirror."

They paddled out of the long cove and turned southwest, skimming close to the steep shore. Overhead a million stars chinked the night sky, and as they paddled Jem picked out Orion's Belt: the three bright studs all in a row and the silver point of the sword that dropped below the belt. There were stars, there was the slender mahogany needle, and there was the dip of the paddle. Jem felt part of it all. It was hard to tell where he left off and the boat began. Wood, water, paddler,

and stars, they combined for night gliding around the island. Soon Jem noticed a stream of stars streaking back from the bow. Each paddle dip produced a galaxy of small, luminous specks, all sliding smoothly astern.

"Phosphorescence!" Ben said. "Stars in the sky! Stars in the water!"

Star paddler, Jem thought, as he dipped his paddle in the water.

They had just rounded the southeast tip of No Name Island when Jem felt the presence of something else in the

water. Catching his breath, he saw, amid the galaxies of phosphorescence, a streaking in the night sea like licks of pale fire.

"Dolphins, Dad!" A pair of dolphins swam just off *Wasso*'s starboard (right) side. Amid the showering sparks of phosphorescence, Jem couldn't really see their shapes. Only the trail of watery fire that streamed around the dolphins was visible.

"They probably think we're a new fish in the neighborhood," said Ben. "Watch them play around us."

The dolphins dived and arced over one another, braiding the bright water, swimming alongside, just out of the dip of the paddles. A magical energy seemed to surround the kayak.

Jem and his dad did not put up their tent that night. The moon was riding high when they passed the last knuckle of the long-fingered cove. The night air was warm and they decided to sleep out instead of covering up the stars. Jem crawled into his sleeping bag feeling a little bit hungry. He realized suddenly that he had never gone to bed feeling a little bit hungry in his life. Tomorrow he would get up early and try to catch a bigger mackerel for breakfast. He didn't need food now, really. Besides, munching hardtack would be too noisy and he wanted to think about things—like his driftwood whale. Why had the sea made a perfect whale? How had it happened? What joining of water, wind, and current had modeled the wood into the unmistakable folds of a whale's eye? What accidental collision of natural forces had shaped the whale's body? Had it taken eleven years? An old person's lifetime? A century? Or a thousand years for wind and water to make the wooden whale? Jem fell asleep thinking of driftwood whales and paddling the stars.

5

Mist rose from the still water of the cove. It was the in-between time, just at the tail end of the last gray of a fading night, but before the first pink of dawn. His father still slept, while Jem stood on a rock with his fishing line. There was a reasonable-sized mackerel in the pail, but Jem was hungry enough that it seemed like a good idea to try for another one. There was a tug on the line. He reeled it in. A plump mackerel thrashed on the end, gilded by the sun that was just slipping up in the east.

Ben was up now, bending over the fire, poking in some kindling to bring it back to life. Jem cleaned the fish on the rock and brought them over to the fire.

"Roe!" That was the first word spoken that morning.

"One of them has roe, Dad." Fish eggs were a favorite of Jem's. He usually liked them with bacon. But this wasn't usual, so he guessed he would like them without.

It would be time to go soon, to leave No Name Island, to paddle out of the long-fingered surprise of a cove. There was a part of Jem that wanted to go—to tell Michael and Jessica and his mother about the galaxies in the water, to show them the driftwood whale. But there was a bigger part that wanted to stay, that wanted the trip never to end.

They washed their dishes with sea water and sand. They packed up their sleeping bags, the fishing gear, their plates and pots and pans. The clam shells and fishbones they returned to the sea. The orange peel and empty instant grape juice can they put in a bag to carry with them. They doused the fire with water and a paddleful of sand. Before they left, Ben set up the camera on self-timing and took a picture of the two of them standing with their paddles at the tip of the finger cove called Surprise on No Name Island.

Summer, which always seemed to gallop from August to Labor Day, had briefly stopped for Jem and his dad. Now they put on their spray skirts and slipped *Wasso* into the water. Jem didn't want to leave. It wasn't just the island he didn't want to leave, it was everything since yesterday morning.

Jem lowered himself into the stern seat. There was that first motion of water under the keel. The thrill was stronger. The boat came alive in a new way for Jem. Everything did seem possible. In that moment he knew that he was not leaving anything behind. None of it—not the peace of the island, not the magic of the dolphins, or the small water galaxies of the night glide, or the skill to chart a course. It was all part of him now, forever, and would be a part of his winter dreams.

As they paddled out of the long-fingered cove, past the first knuckle and the second, Jem began to dream a new dream—the dream for summers to come, when his parents would let go, when he and Michael would be old enough to paddle alone to another island for a day, a week, or maybe a summer of a thousand miles.

South Porcupine